The Duet

ii

The Duet

by
Brenda Silsbe

Illustrated by Galan Akin

A Hodgepog Book

Hodgepog Books acknowledges the ongoing support of the Canada Council for the Arts and the Alberta foundation for the Arts for our publishing program. We also acknowledge the support of the City of Edmonton and the Edmonton Arts Council.

Editors: Luanne Armstrong, Dorothy Woodend & Amanda Gibbs

Cover design by Linda Uyehara Hoffman
Inside layout by Linda Uyehara Hoffman
Set in Palatino and Helvetica in Quark XPress 4.1
Printed at Hignell Book Printing

A Hodgepog Book for Kids

Published in Canada by Hodgepog Books,
3476 Tupper Street
Vancouver, BC
V5Z 3B7
Telephone (604) 874-1167
Fax (604) 681-1431
Email: dorothy@axion.net

Canadian Cataloguing in Publication Data

Silsbe, Brenda 1953
The Duet

ISBN 0-9686899-1-4

I. Akin, Galan 1968-II. Title.

PS8587.I268D83 2000   JC813'.54   C00-900874-8
PZ7.S5854Du 2000

To everyone who taught me anything about music,
with much gratitude

vi

Contents

Chapter One
Sister Decides

Maggie walked toward the convent, hugging her music books close to her chest. Maggie was frowning. Maggie had a problem.

Last week, Sister Bernadette had asked Maggie if she wanted to play a piano piece in the Spring Music Festival.

"You don't have to decide today," Sister Bernadette had said. "Think about it. You can give me an answer next week."

Maggie couldn't stop thinking about it. All week she worried.

Maggie didn't want to play in the Festival. If she played in the Festival, she would have to play in front of an adjudicator and an audience. The adjudicator would mark her and she would have to compete against the other kids. Just thinking about it made Maggie nervous.

But Maggie didn't know how to say no to Sister Bernadette. Maggie found it hard to say no to most people. How could she say no to a nun?

A few stragglers from the Catholic School were throwing snowballs in the schoolyard. Maggie kept an eye on them. After all, she was a stranger here.

As soon as Maggie pushed open the big, front door of the convent, she smelled fresh bread.

Baking day, thought Maggie.

Maggie walked down the tiled stairs and along the dark hall to the music room. She heard the sound of the piano through the closed door. It must be the red-haired girl from the Catholic School. Her lesson always came before Maggie's.

Whoops! The red-haired girl made a mistake. The line of music was played over and over until the notes were right. Sister Bernadette never ignored a mistake.

Maggie sat down on the shiny oak bench opposite the door. She imagined saying no to Sister Bernadette. She imagined Sister Bernadette smiling sweetly and replying, "Okay." How Maggie wished that would happen!

Soon there was silence. Maggie heard Sister Bernadette's soft voice. Then the door opened.

The red-haired girl came out first. Her bangs were sticking straight out, her cheeks were flushed and her eyes were very round. Maggie didn't think that the red-haired girl liked playing the piano. Perhaps her mother and father forced her to take lessons.

"Good-bye, Sister," said the red-haired girl. She made a quick get-away down the hall and up the stairs.

Sister Bernadette smiled and waved good-bye. Then she turned to Maggie.

"Come along, dear," she said.

Maggie followed the minty smell and swishing robes of the nun. Perhaps it was different for the red-haired girl, being Catholic and all, but Maggie was in awe of Sister Bernadette. In fact, Maggie was amazed by everything in the convent: the quiet sisters, their black robes, the beautiful statues standing in every corner.

"Let me hear your scales, please," said Sister Bernadette, sitting gracefully on her chair and folding her soft, plump hands on her lap.

Maggie began her scales. She played triads and exercises. Then she did three songs. Maggie was more nervous than usual; she made many mistakes. Every time Maggie made a mistake, Sister Bernadette clicked her tongue or shook her head.

"You must practice more, my dear," said Sister Bernadette.

"Yes, Sister," said Maggie.

Maggie wanted to say, I do practice! I do! I know these songs; I can play them perfectly at home. It's only when I get in front of people, especially you, Sister Bernadette, that I can't play them. Then my fingers become stiff and clumsy and I forget all the notes.

But Maggie didn't say that because she was a little afraid of Sister Bernadette and because she thought it might be rude.

At the end of Maggie's lesson, Sister Bernadette said, "Maggie, do you remember what I asked you last week?"

"Yes," replied Maggie cautiously.

"Have you decided?" asked Sister Bernadette.

Maggie felt the blood drain from her face.

"I don't really want to play in the Festival, Sister Bernadette," whispered Maggie.

Sister Bernadette looked at the piano.

"I think it will be good for you," said Sister Bernadette.

"But I get nervous playing in front of people," said Maggie.

"Then it will be good practice for you," said Sister Bernadette cheerfully.

Maggie sighed. She didn't know what else to say.

"Perhaps," said Sister Bernadette gently, "you

could play a duet. Kathleen Brown, the girl whose lesson comes before yours, is also nervous about playing in the Festival. I know a duet that would be just right for both of you."

Maggie wanted to say no but she didn't know how. And she didn't want to hurt Sister Bernadette's feelings. Maybe, she reasoned, a duet wasn't as bad as a solo.

"All right," replied Maggie reluctantly.

Sister Bernadette smiled.

"I'll have your copy of the duet by next week. You can learn your own part first. Then you and Kathleen can practice together. I will arrange extra practice times at the convent for you."

Maggie nodded.

Sister Bernadette walked Maggie to the front door and waved good-bye as Maggie walked slowly across the playground. Maggie waved back. She tried to smile but her heart was heavy. Oh, if only she had the courage to say no!

Chapter Two
Maggie Alone

A pot lid danced noisily on the Stone family stove. Maggie's older sister, Wanda, was singing in her bedroom; her younger brother, David, was watching television in the living room. Maggie put her music books on the piano bench. Dad was stirring gravy on the stove so Maggie wandered into the kitchen.

"How was your lesson?" asked Dad.

"It was okay," replied Maggie.

Dad raised his eyebrows.

"Just okay?" he asked.

"I have to play in the Festival," said Maggie.

"That's great," began Dad. Then he noticed

Maggie's wrinkled nose. "Don't you want to play in the Festival?"

Maggie frowned. "No," she answered.

"Why not?" asked Dad.

"I don't like playing in front of people. It makes me nervous."

"You play in front of us," said Dad.

"That's different," argued Maggie.

"No, it's not," said Dad. "All you have to do is pretend that the audience is full of family and friends and play like you do at home."

Maggie groaned.

"Nobody understands," she said.

"Nobody understands what?" asked Mom, coming through the kitchen door. Mom put down her brief-case. She kissed Maggie and she kissed Dad.

Dad explained Maggie's problem — except that it didn't sound like a problem when Dad told it.

Mom smiled and patted Maggie's cheek.

"You'll do fine, Maggie."

Maggie wasn't sure about that. She thought about talking it over with Wanda. But Wanda wouldn't understand. Wanda had been playing in the Festival for years. She actually thought it was fun. Maggie sighed. Wanda was good at everything. She got A's where Maggie got B's and she never had to study for those A's either. Maggie had to work hard for every B. Wanda's hair was shiny, dark brown, thick and long; Maggie's hair was thin and mousey. Wanda was even good at sports. Maggie wished she had Wanda's confidence. Maybe when she was twelve she would turn into a Wanda. But now she was only nine and she was scaredy-cat Maggie through and through.

At dinner, David turned to Wanda and said, "Maggie's scared to play in the Festival."

"David!" exclaimed Mom and Dad at the same time.

Wanda shrugged her shoulders. "There's nothing to be afraid of," she said.

"Easy for you to say," mumbled Maggie.

That night, Maggie dreamed about being on the stage at the Festival. She had forgotten her music, she was dressed in her pajamas and she couldn't remember the song she was supposed to play.

Kathleen was sitting in the audience and wouldn't come up on the stage. Everyone was laughing at her. What a terrible dream!

The next morning, David pretended to play the piano whenever he saw Maggie.

"You wait until it's your turn," said Maggie.

"I'm not gonna do it if I don't want to," said David.

Maggie looked at David's determined little mouth and believed him. David was a brick. If only she had his courage.

Maggie and David walked to school together. David whistled and chased cats and kicked rocks as if the world was a happy place. But Maggie couldn't enjoy anything with the dreaded duet hanging over her head. She didn't even get upset when David shook a cedar branch and snow fell on her head.

"You're no fun," said David.

At school, Maggie told her best friends, Michelle and Brianna, about the Festival. They thought it was wonderful news. They were going to be in the Festival too. What if one of them got a first! Brianna did speech arts; Michelle sang. Maggie thought that both of those would be easier than playing the piano.

"Speech arts isn't easy," protested Brianna. "You have to memorize a whole poem and breathe right and not wiggle and the adjudicator always thinks of something you did wrong."

"But if your hands sweat, you can hide them," said Maggie.

"What if your voice stops working?" asked Brianna. "I squeaked once."

Michelle giggled.

"Yah," she said, "once my throat got all dry and I sounded like a bullfrog."

Maggie was unconvinced.

That day, Mrs. Jenkins announced that their class would be either reciting a poem or singing a song in the Music Festival. The class would vote on it.

Brianna voted for a poem; Michelle voted for a song. Maggie didn't care what they did. Anything would be easier than playing a piano duet with a stranger.

Maggie wondered about Kathleen Brown. What was she like? Would she be nice or snobby? Where would they practice together?

Maggie stared out the classroom window. There isn't one person who understands how I feel, thought Maggie. Not one!

Chapter Three
First Practice

All that week, Maggie thought about the duet and Kathleen Brown.

At the next lesson, Maggie stared at Kathleen as she and Sister Bernadette came out of the music room. Kathleen glanced quickly at Maggie. Kathleen seemed embarrassed and nervous.

When Sister Bernadette handed Maggie the duet music, Maggie's stomach felt like it was full of hot rocks.

She wished she could say, "I've changed my mind, Sister. I don't want to play in the Music Festival."

But all she said was, "Thank you, Sister," and stared at the music sheets.

The duet wasn't hard. Maggie could play it fairly well by the third week. That was the week when she and Kathleen would practice together for the first time. Kathleen was going to stay an extra fifteen minutes and play the duet with Maggie. Then Maggie's lesson would go half an hour past that.

As she waited on the oak bench outside the music room, Maggie was curious to know how they would sound together. She had tried Kathleen's part — she had tried to imagine the parts together — but she just couldn't hear the duet in her head.

The music stopped. The door opened. Sister Bernadette appeared, smiled at Maggie and said, "Come in."

Maggie entered the music room and slowly hung up her coat. Kathleen sat hunched on the piano bench, her hair messy and her cheeks flushed.

"Sit up straight, Kathleen," said Sister Bernadette. "Move to the right so that Maggie can sit down."

Kathleen sat up straight; Kathleen moved over. She looked at Maggie with wide eyes. Maggie looked back. Maggie suddenly realized that Kathleen didn't want to play in the Festival any more than she did. Maggie smiled at Kathleen and shrugged her shoulders. Kathleen smiled shyly back.

Although Maggie had practiced her part over and over, she wasn't sure how well she could play it if another person pounded out a different part right beside her. Sometimes, when Maggie was singing a song, Wanda would start to harmonize and Maggie couldn't sing the right notes any more. It was hard to concentrate. It made her even more nervous with Sister Bernadette watching carefully from behind.

"Ready, girls?" asked Sister Bernadette. Then she counted, "One, two, one, two."

Kathleen started to play. Maggie froze. Maggie had missed the beginning and didn't know where to jump in.

Sister Bernadette tapped her pencil on the side of the piano. Kathleen stopped playing.

Sister Bernadette leaned between the girls, smelling of mint and soap. She put her hands in Maggie's position and said,"Watch and listen carefully, Maggie. Start again, Kathleen. One, two, one, two."

After Sister Bernadette showed Maggie how to start the duet, the practice went on without a major mistake. After fifteen minutes, Kathleen looked exhausted, Maggie was a nervous wreck and Sister Bernadette was very quiet. Finally Sister Bernadette said, "That was lovely, girls."

Kathleen and Maggie looked at each other in surprise.

Sister Bernadette handed a sheet of paper to each girl. "Here are the days and times when you can practice at the convent. It would be nice if you could practice at each other's houses too. That will be all,

Kathleen. You may go."

Kathleen ran a sweaty hand through her bangs.

That's why Kathleen's hair is always sticking up! thought Maggie.

"I don't know Maggie's phone number," said Kathleen quietly.

"I'll write it down for you," said Maggie, scribbling her full name and phone number on Kathleen's schedule. Then she handed the pencil to Kathleen.

"Could you please give me yours?"

Kathleen hurriedly wrote down her name and phone number. Then she grabbed her coat, hat and music books and, after mumbling a quick good-bye, slipped out the door.

She's very shy, thought Maggie.

"You may begin with your scales," said Sister Bernadette.

Maggie concentrated on the keyboard and forgot about the duet and Kathleen – at least for a few minutes. She had plenty of time to think about them on the windy, cold walk home.

Chapter Four
Tell Me

Maggie liked the sound that her boots made on the dry snow. Everything was pretty after last night's snowfall. Thin white lines balanced on black branches, old snow piles looked new. Maggie was meeting Kathleen at the convent for their first practice without Sister Bernadette.

When Maggie arrived at the music room, Kathleen was waiting for her.

"You're lucky that you go to school here," said Maggie, taking off her coat and blowing on her hands. "I had to walk six blocks and my fingers are nearly frozen."

"I guess," responded Kathleen. "But you don't have Sister Bernadette as your Art and Gym teacher."

"Gym teacher?" Maggie was stunned. She tried to imagine Sister Bernadette playing basketball. She couldn't do it!

Kathleen nodded her head.

"That's weird," said Maggie.

Maggie put her sheet music on the piano ledge.

"Do you like piano lessons?" she asked Kathleen.

Kathleen hesitated. "No," she said. "I mean, it's nice to be able to play the piano but taking lessons from your school teacher isn't fun. It was Mom's idea anyway. I wanted to play the guitar."

Kathleen stared sadly at the eighty-eight keys in front of her. Then she looked at Maggie. "Do *you* like piano lessons?"

"Sure. But I don't like playing in front of anybody. And I don't want to play in the Festival."

"Neither do I!" said Kathleen. "But what can we do about it?"

Maggie sighed. "I guess we're stuck with it," she said.

Kathleen nodded. There seemed to be nothing more to say so they counted two bars and started their duet. Maggie usually hated practice. Practice was boring. But this time it was different. Every time they made a mistake, instead of getting angry or frustrated, the girls laughed and joked and tried again. Every time they played a passage right, they would clap and cheer and congratulate each other. Maggie and Kathleen were enjoying themselves so much that they even went over their practice time. The boy who was using the room after them had to knock on the door and remind them that their time was up.

Maggie discovered that Kathleen lived three blocks east of the convent. Kathleen's house was on Maggie's way home. So the girls walked back together. They walked slowly and talked quickly.

After they discussed practice times, Maggie asked Kathleen all sorts of questions about the Catholic School and the Catholic Church. Maggie asked about the statues, the nuns, the school uniforms. She wanted to know what "Our Lady of the Sacred Heart" meant.

"What church do you go to?" asked Kathleen.

`"We don't go to church," said Maggie.

Kathleen was shocked. "You don't go to any church?"

Kathleen made it sound like any church was better than no church at all. Maggie laughed. "No," she answered, unperturbed.

For a moment Kathleen was speechless. Then she said, "What about your friends?"

Maggie thought. "Brianna's dad is a Baptist minister and Michelle's dad is Jewish and Michelle's mom meditates. That's all I know."

"Hmmm," said Kathleen.

Then they talked about movies and pets and their favourite books. They both liked mysteries, especially Eric Wilson mysteries. Maggie was so glad to find someone who liked the same books that she liked. Brianna and Michelle were great fun for games but they didn't like reading. Before the girls knew it,they were in front of Kathleen's house. It was much smaller than Maggie's house but it had a bigger yard.

"My mom likes to garden," explained Kathleen.

"My mom hates to garden," said Maggie.

They both laughed.

"I'll see you later," said Maggie as Kathleen opened the gate.

Maggie was sorry to say good-bye. It was fun talking with Kathleen. Kathleen could talk about anything. She wasn't shy after all.

"Practice at your house on Thursday?" asked Kathleen.

"Right!" answered Maggie.

As soon as Kathleen disappeared into the house, Maggie pulled up her collar. She and Kathleen had been so busy talking that she hadn't noticed how cold it was. As Maggie trudged home she thought, "Three blocks with a friend goes faster than three blocks by myself."

Maggie missed the laughter and conversation. The only sound now was the hoarse caw of a crow and the lonely squeak and crunch of dry snow under Maggie's boots.

Chapter Five
Home Practice

On Thursday, Kathleen went to Maggie's house. As soon as Kathleen walked through the front door, she was astonished by the noise.

Wanda was typing a report in her bedroom, David was playing rock and roll in the living room, Maggie's dad was hammering and sawing in the basement and Maggie's mom was in the kitchen chopping food, crashing pots and singing along with the radio.

Wanda pounded on the wall and yelled, "David! Turn that music down!"

David, of course, couldn't hear her.

Maggie's mom hollered down the heating vent, "Eric! Where's the good knife? Did you take it fishing again?"

"My house is never this noisy!" laughed Kathleen, taking off her coat and hat.

"How many brothers and sisters do you have?" asked Maggie.

"None," answered Kathleen.

"None?" exclaimed Maggie. "You're an only child?"

"Almost," said Kathleen. "I have a half-brother and a half-sister at my dad's house."

"Your dad's house?"

"Yes," replied Kathleen. "My mom and dad were

divorced when I was three. Dad got married again and has two more kids. My mom and I live together — just the two of us. It's very quiet."

"Oh," said Maggie. She led Kathleen to the rec room. "I'll shut the door while we practice. You won't be able to concentrate if I leave it open."

Kathleen laughed.

The practice went well. The duet was beginning to sound like a duet instead of two solos being played at the same time.

"Maybe we'll do okay at the Festival," said Kathleen.

"Easy to say in the rec room with the door closed!" said Maggie.

Dad opened the door. "Can you take a break?" he asked. "I've made popcorn."

Maggie looked at Kathleen. "Popcorn?"

Kathleen smiled and nodded her head.

"Let's go!" said Maggie and the girls raced upstairs, leaving their music sheets perched uneasily on the piano.

When Maggie went to Kathleen's house, she was almost afraid to talk. A chime clock ticked quietly on the mantel, sheer curtains on the windows created a muted light in the house and thick carpets seemed to swallow their footsteps.

"What time does your mother come home?" asked Maggie hopefully.

"At four," said Kathleen.

With nothing to distract them, the girls started to practice right away. Maggie had the feeling that at any moment someone would run down the stairs or out of a room and go, SHHH!

The girls didn't laugh as much at Kathleen's house as they did at Maggie's but they were able to concentrate better and they felt as if they had greatly improved their duet by the time Kathleen's mother walked through the front door.

Mrs. Brown applauded. "Encore!" she cried. "One more time!"

Kathleen and Maggie smiled at each other. "One, two, one two!"

The girls started to play with confidence. But the more Maggie thought about Kathleen's mother watching them, the more her fingers fumbled over her notes. Then Kathleen's timing went off. The duet fell apart after that although the girls managed to struggle to the end. Mrs. Brown was full of compliments but Maggie and Kathleen felt downhearted and discouraged.

"Do you think we'll ever be able to do it right for the Festival?" asked Kathleen.

"I don't know," replied Maggie glumly.

"Of course you will!" Kathleen's mom called from the front hall.

The girls looked at each other with doubtful expressions. If only they could believe her!

Chapter Six
The Day

When Maggie changed her three calendars to March, she got a queasy feeling in her stomach. The Festival was only two weeks away!

Maggie and Kathleen had practiced as much as they could, but Maggie still felt uneasy about playing on stage in front of an audience.

"At least we can play in front of Sister Bernadette without making a mistake," said Kathleen.

"Yes," agreed Maggie. "*That's* something. But I hope Sister Bernadette isn't disappointed in us if we make a mistake at the Festival."

"She has so many pupils," replied Kathleen. "I'm sure she's not putting all her hopes on us!"

Maggie recalled the proud look on Sister Bernadette's face when the girls managed to play the duet all the way through without a mistake.

"I'm not so sure," said Maggie.

When they weren't worrying about the Festival, Maggie and Kathleen had a great time together. They seemed to think the same way. They liked the same jokes.They played the same games. Kathleen was getting used to noisy houses and Maggie was starting to appreciate quiet ones. There was only one black cloud over their friendship and it was moving in fast.

On the morning of her Festival performance, Maggie couldn't eat.

"You have to eat something," said Mom.

"I can't," said Maggie.

"How about pickles and onions and liver with pig's eyeballs?" asked David.

Maggie ignored him.

"What time do you play?" asked Dad.

"At one o'clock," said Maggie.

"I wish I didn't have that meeting," said Dad.

"I could still get time off," said Mom.

Maggie shook her head. "Really — I don't want you to come."

Mom looked hurt and Maggie felt sorry. But they had already talked about it. Maggie didn't want them to come because it made her even more nervous.

"Next time?" asked Mom.

Maggie nodded but she hoped there wouldn't be a next time. Maggie turned to Wanda. "Are you nervous?" she asked. Wanda was also playing in the Festival today.

"A little," said Wanda. "But once I start playing, I forget how nervous I am. You'll see. It'll be okay."

Maggie wished that Wanda was right but wishing didn't erase her doubts.

Brianna and Michelle didn't recite or sing until next week so Maggie was all alone with her nerves. Her schoolmates seemed unaware that her life was about to end. How could they run and play and laugh at recess when Maggie was going to meet her doom?

Maggie left school at noon. She tried to eat her jam and peanut butter sandwich on the way to the Catholic School but she still wasn't hungry. Maggie was glad that Kathleen was waiting for her on the sidewalk beside the playground. Maggie couldn't face a strange school right now. Kathleen's face was white and her hair looked redder than ever.

"Oh, Maggie," said Kathleen. "I'm glad we're doing this together. I hope I'm not going to be sick. I felt like staying home this morning but I knew that you and Sister Bernadette were counting on me."

Maggie laughed. She told Kathleen about her "Festival" dream.

"I've had the same dream about ten times. This morning I made sure that I had my music, that I wasn't wearing my pyjamas and that I knew what song I was going to play. I really don't think the audience will laugh at us. So the only thing I have to worry about is if you will come up on stage with me. I'd look pretty silly playing the second part all by myself."

"Oh, don't worry," said Kathleen. "I'll go up with you — even if you have to carry me!"

At the auditorium, Maggie and Kathleen had to wait in the lobby until the last group of performers finished playing. Kathleen curled and uncurled her music sheets with her sweaty hands.

When the music stopped, Maggie and Kathleen were allowed to enter the auditorium.

"There are more people coming in than going out," Maggie whispered to Kathleen in dismay.

Inside the hall, the group that had entered with the girls quickly and quietly found seats. Maggie and Kathleen remained in the aisle staring at the big, shiny, black grand piano that stood on the stage.

Maggie looked around at the other children. The girls were dressed in frills and patent leather shoes; the boys wore fine suits and smart ties. Maggie felt out of place in her dowdy, grey skirt and plain white blouse. She felt better, however, when Kathleen moaned.

"I wish I wasn't wearing this dumb uniform!"

"You look great," Maggie whispered. "Don't worry."

A well-dressed woman sat at a desk in the middle

of the auditorium, writing on papers and studying sheets of music.

"That must be the adjudicator," said Maggie. Now *Maggie's* hands began to sweat. The adjudicator scared her more than Sister Bernadette.

Kathleen and Maggie had no idea where they were supposed to sit or what they were supposed to do so they quickly found some seats at the back of the auditorium and watched and listened.

Soon the adjudicator gathered up her papers and swept down to the front of the hall. She smiled sweetly at the children who had just played the piano.

"My!" she said dramatically. "What wonderful performances! You *have* practiced hard, haven't you?"

The adjudicator then launched into a long description of what the young pianists had accomplished and how they did it and how they could improve. She gave out certificates, pinched the cheeks of the children and told jokes to the audience.

She likes being on stage, thought Maggie.

Then the adjudicator waltzed up the stairs to her desk while the children in the front row dispersed, all of them looking depressed except the ones who got first and second. One boy was even crying!

The adjudicator's assistant stood up and announced the next class.

"That's us!" cried Maggie.

"What are we supposed to do?" asked Kathleen.

Maggie watched the other children. They were marching down to the front.

"Come on," whispered Maggie. She grabbed Kathleen's arm and hurried to the aisle. Maggie and Kathleen were the last of their class to be seated. Maggie looked down the row. She and Kathleen were like ruffled wrens in a line of swans. The only difference between her and a wren was that the wren could fly away.

Chapter Seven
The Performance

The silence strained Maggie's nerves. What was the adjudicator doing up there? Why did they have to wait so long?

Maggie stared at the grand piano looming in front of her on the wide stage. She had never played a grand piano before. Were grand pianos different from other pianos? Maggie noticed that the piano was facing right. That meant that Kathleen would have to sit on the side nearest the audience. Poor Kathleen!

Once Maggie went to see Wanda play in the Festival. But she was sure it hadn't taken this long. Of course, Mom brought peppermints and Maggie brought a puzzlebook. If only she had a peppermint now! All that Maggie and Kathleen could do was stare at the grand piano and twiddle their fingers.

Maggie was thirsty. Her throat was dry. Now she knew what Brianna and Michelle felt like. Maggie remembered that Wanda sometimes wore gloves to keep her hands warm. Maggie's hands were warm and sweaty. *She* didn't need gloves. Maggie rubbed her hands on her skirt.

The silence was broken. The assistant called some names. Two boys hurried up the stage stairs, plopped noisily down on the piano bench and pounded out a duet with steady fingers. Their playing wasn't artistic but they made no mistakes. Maggie crossed her fingers. She hoped that she and Kathleen could play as surely and steadily as those two boys.

When the boys finished, they bowed quickly and returned to their seats. There was a long pause.

The assistant called more names. Two girls, beautifully dressed, tripped up the stairs and arranged themselves nicely on the piano bench. The girls played prettily, with only two or three mistakes, and curtsied most charmingly when they were finished. The audience went, "Aw!"

Then, after another long silence, the assistant called, "Margaret Stone and Kathleen Brown."

Maggie heard Kathleen's stomach gurgle. Kathleen heard Maggie swallow. They clumped and bumped up the five stairs to the stage. Maggie felt like an elephant walking in slow motion as she plodded over to the piano.

Kathleen slid into her spot and Maggie sat beside her. As the girls adjusted the piano bench, its legs

made a loud scraping, screeching sound that echoed throughout the hall. They placed their music sheets on the piano's shiny ledge. Kathleen wiped her hands on her navy blue skirt. Maggie swallowed again. Why was her mouth so dry?

"Whenever you're ready, girls," said the adjudicator in a sugar-coated voice. Maggie knew that if someone said "whenever you're ready" they didn't really mean "whenever you're ready" — they meant "Hurry up!"

Maggie whispered, "One, two, one, two," and the girls started to play.

After the first bar, Maggie was in shock. The keys of the grand piano were difficult to press down. She had to hit them twice as hard as the keys on her own piano. Maggie wondered if Kathleen was having the same trouble.

Keep playing, Maggie told herself. Here comes the third line. One mistake, two mistakes. Stop counting mistakes! Keep playing.

Then it happened.

Kathleen's music sheet, the sheet she had curled and uncurled in the lobby, came sliding down over the shiny, black ledge and landed neatly on top of their hands.

They stopped playing. Maggie looked at Kathleen; Kathleen stared at the sheet. There wasn't a sound in the hall, no coughing, no whispering, no scratch of the adjudicator's pencil.

Maggie was so nervous and shaky that it took her a whole thirty seconds to get Kathleen's sheet back on the ledge. Kathleen's face was as red as strawberries and her neck was all blotchy. Kathleen's hand went instinctively up through her bangs. Her bangs stood straight up.

Maggie had an overwhelming desire to laugh. She knew she mustn't. But this was one thing she never expected and it seemed so funny.

Kathleen whispered, "One, two, one, two," and the girls started the duet again.

They never made it to the second line. Both sheets of music came down this time, sliding over Kathleen and Maggie's hands on their way to the floor. Maggie grabbed and Kathleen dived and they bumped heads.

"Ow!

"Ouch!"

Maggie tried to stifle a laugh and ended up snorting. As soon as she snorted, Kathleen started to giggle. Then they didn't know what was worse: trying to get those sheets to stay on the narrow ledge or trying to stop laughing.

Finally, the adjudicator, in a voice like ice, said, "You may sit down, girls."

Oh, the embarrassment! Oh, the disgrace! As Maggie and Kathleen hurried to their seats, Maggie glanced at the audience. All the mothers, fathers, aunts, uncles and grandparents in the hall looked horrified. What if their children did something so terrible? It was as if they thought bad behaviour was catching. Most of the children in the auditorium looked scared. What if it happened to them?

Maggie and Kathleen tried to stop laughing. They held their breath and put their hands over their mouths. They didn't look at each other. Maggie was sure if she saw Kathleen's bangs one more time she would become hysterical. But every time someone else got up and played a duet, Maggie and Kathleen would think of those sheets falling and it would start them off again. It wasn't until Maggie saw Sister Bernadette at the far right of the auditorium that she managed to control herself. Sister Bernadette looked so disappointed.

When the adjudicator came down to the front to discuss their performances, she didn't say much about Maggie and Kathleen. Not that it mattered very much: Maggie couldn't remember a thing the adjudicator said to anybody. When the adjudicator handed them their adjudication sheet, neither Maggie nor Kathleen felt like reading the comments.

The girls left the hall as quickly as possible. Maggie was glad that her mother and father hadn't been there for the performance. She was also glad that she didn't have to face Sister Bernadette until next Monday.

Maggie and Kathleen discussed every detail of the performance on the way back to the Catholic School. Talking about it made them both feel better.

"I'm glad you were there!" said Maggie.

"I'm glad you were there too," said Kathleen.

Kathleen paused at the gate of the school grounds. "Do you want to come over after school on Friday?"

"Sure," replied Maggie. "And we won't have to practice piano!"

"Right!"

Kathleen waved good-bye and Maggie waved back. Then Maggie started the long walk back to her own school. She was relieved that the performance was over. Yet she felt embarrassed and uncomfortable. She didn't know how to tell her family and she dreaded facing Sister Bernadette. Now Maggie wished that Monday was tomorrow: she wanted that meeting to be over!

Chapter Eight
Final Twists

When Maggie told her family about the Festival, Mom and Dad were sympathetic.

"I'm sure you did your best, dear," said Mom.

"I once laughed in church," said Dad. "And your grandpa hauled me out by my ear."

"You used to go to church?" asked Maggie in astonishment.

"That was a long time ago," laughed Dad. "We were supposed to sit very still in church. We couldn't make any noise and we had to listen to every word the preacher said. One day I couldn't stand it any more. The preacher said something sad. Some people cried. Everyone looked mournful — except me. I burst out laughing. Grandpa was so angry. But I really couldn't help it."

David was all ears. "Did you get a spanking, Dad?"

"No," said Dad. "Grandpa didn't believe in spankings. But I had to apologize to the preacher — and that was worse!"

"I bet nothing like this every happened to Wanda," said Maggie.

Wanda blushed. "Oh, yes it did. Except I never told anyone."

All eyes were on Wanda.

"In Grade Three, my teacher asked me to play my Festival piece at an assembly. You were in Kindergarten, Maggie, and you had already gone home. When I sat down at the piano, I suddenly sneezed. It was awful. There was snot all over the piano keys."

"Gross!" yelled David.

"I didn't want to touch it so I just ran off the stage. I still don't know who cleaned it up."

David started to laugh and soon everyone was laughing, even Wanda.

"These things happen to everyone," said Mom.

"I hope it never happens to me," said David.

"It will!" insisted Wanda.

On Monday, Maggie went unwillingly to piano lessons. As she slowly walked along the muddy streets, Maggie wondered how Sister Bernadette could possibly understand. Nuns didn't have children. Nuns were always well-behaved. Nuns lived perfect lives — at least, that's what Maggie believed. Perhaps Sister Bernadette remembered what it was like to be a child. But no — that was too long ago. Maggie wondered if nuns were allowed to giggle or laugh. They smiled, of course, but that was different.

Maggie arrived at the convent just as Kathleen finished her lesson. Sister Bernadette was out in the hall with Kathleen so Maggie couldn't find out what had happened during the lesson. Kathleen and Maggie exchanged sympathetic looks.

Then Maggie went into the music room with Sister Bernadette. Maggie put her music books on the piano bench and took off her coat while Sister Bernadette waited patiently.

When Maggie slid onto the bench, she said, "I know you are disappointed, Sister. I'm sorry we ruined the duet and I'm sorry we laughed."

Maggie looked down at her hands. When Sister Bernadette didn't say anything, Maggie looked up. Why, Sister Bernadette's eyes were twinkling!

"My dear," began Sister Bernadette. "It was wrong of me to pressure you to go into the Festival when you didn't want to. I didn't realize that you meant it when you said no. Some people need a little nudging. Some people want to go into the Festival but they lack courage, they want encouragement. I thought you were one of those people. I was wrong. It is I who should apologize to you."

"No, Sister," protested Maggie.

"Oh, yes, Maggie," laughed Sister Bernadette. "And I must tell you — you both did an excellent job on that duet — even if your families and I were the only ones who heard it. I'm proud of you for working together and for practicing so hard."

Because she was expecting criticism and got praise instead, Maggie didn't know what to say. "Thank you, Sister," she mumbled.

"Did you read what the adjudicator said?" asked Sister Bernadette.

Maggie shook her head. It was bad enough that she could imagine what the adjudicator said.

"Kathleen gave me the sheet with her comments. Here." Sister Bernadette gave the sheet to Maggie.

Maggie read:"I would like these girls to try again next year. They had a strong start and when they get over their nervousness, they will be fine musicians."

Maggie blushed and Sister Bernadette smiled.

"Shall we start with your scales?"

Maggie put her hands in position. Then she turned to Sister Bernadette. "Sister," said Maggie, "did you see the look on the adjudicator's face when we started to laugh?"

Sister Bernadette put her hand to her mouth. She didn't make a sound but her shoulders shook and she silently laughed so hard that tears came to her eyes.

Maggie laughed too.

Maggie made few mistakes that day and Sister Bernadette was pleased with the lesson.

When Maggie left the convent, Kathleen was waiting for her on the playground. They walked home together and talked about Sister Bernadette's reaction to the Festival.

"I guess there's more to Sister Bernadette than meets the eye," said Maggie.

Kathleen nodded her head. Suddenly, she grabbed Maggie's arm.

"Hey! Guess what?" she said. "I asked Mom about guitar lessons again."

"What did she say?" asked Maggie.

Kathleen grinned. "She said, 'In light of your performance in the Festival, it might be a better choice.'"

"What does *that* mean?" asked Maggie.

"It means YES!" laughed Kathleen.

Maggie clapped her hands. "Great!" she said. Then Maggie stopped. She frowned. "Does that mean you won't be taking piano anymore?"

"No more piano!" shouted Kathleen. Then she saw the look on Maggie's face. "But we'll still see each other, right?"

Maggie smiled and nodded her head.

"You know," said Kathleen, "if it hadn't been for piano lessons and this Festival..."

"...we never would have become friends," finished Maggie.

They both smiled.

"I never thought I'd ever say there was something good about playing in the Festival," said Maggie.

"Or piano lessons!" added Kathleen.

They walked a few minutes in silence. Then a small bird in a bare maple tree interrupted their thoughts with a bright, spring song.

Kathleen started to sing her part of the duet:
"Ba da dum dum dum,
Ba da dum dum dum,
Dum dum dum dum da!"

Maggie joined in with her part. The girls sang the duet in tune and in time all the way to Kathleen's house. They weren't nervous when people stared at them and they never made one mistake. If only Sister Bernadette could have heard them. Surely Sister

Bernadette would have said that here, at last, was the perfect duet.

The End

About the Author

Brenda Silsbe lives in Terrace, British Columbia. She received a Bachelor of Education from UBC and taught primary school in Terrace for three years. She still lives in Terrace with her husband John, her daughter Anne and her son Jesse. Brenda first began to write and send out children's stories in 1988. Her first story was published in 1989. She has previously published five children's books. This is her first book for Hodgepog.

About the Illustrator

Galan Akin is an artist and illustrator living in Vancouver, British Columbia. Born in Oakland, California, he grew up on various islands on the west coast of Canada. He studied painting at the Nova Scotia College of Art & Design and animation at the Emily Carr Institute of Art & Design.

If you liked this book...
you might enjoy these other Hodgepog Books:
read them yourself in grades 3–5, or read them to
younger kids.

Ben and the Carrot Predicament
by Mar'ce Merrell, illustrated by Barbara Hartmann
ISBN 1-895836-54-9   Price $4.95

Getting Rid of Mr. Ributus
by Alison Lohans, illustrated by Barbara Hartmann
ISBN 1-895836-53-0   Price $6.95

A Real Farm Girl
By Susan Ioannou, illustrated by James Rozak
ISBN 1-895836-52-2   Price $6.95

A Gift for Johnny Know-It-All
by Mary Woodbury, illustrated by Barbara Hartmann
ISBN 1-895836-27-1   Price $5.95

Mill Creek Kids
by Colleen Heffernan, illustrated by Sonja Zacharias
ISBN 1-895836-40-9   Price $5.95

Arly & Spike
by Luanne Armstrong, illustrated by Chao Yu
ISBN 1-895836-37-9   Price $4.95

A Friend for Mr. Granville
by Gillian Richardson, illustrated by Claudette Maclean
ISBN 1-895836-38-7   Price $5.95

Maggie & Shine
by Luanne Armstrong, illustrated by Dorothy Woodend
ISBN 1-895836-67-0   Price $6.95

Butterfly Gardens
by Judith Benson, illustrated by Lori McGregor McCrae
ISBN 1-895836-71-9   Price $5.95

The Duet
by Brenda Silsbe, illustrated by Galan Akin
ISBN 0-9686899-1-4 $5.95

Jeremy's Christmas Wish
by Glen Huser, illustrated by Martin Rose
ISBN 0-9686899-2-2 $5.95

And for readers in grade 1-2,
or to read to pre-schoolers

Sebastian's Promise
by Gwen Molnar, illustrated by Kendra McCleskey
ISBN 1-895836-65-4   Price $4.95

Summer With Sebastian
by Gwen Molnar, illustrated by Kendra McClesky
ISBN 1-895836-39-5   Price $4.95

The Noise in Grandma's Attic
by Judith Benson, illustrated by Shane Hill
ISBN 1-895836-55-7   Price $4.95

Pet Fair
by Deb Loughead, illustrated by Lisa Birke
ISBN 0-9686899-3-0 $5.95